DALTON'S DREAM

My Ancestors Sailed From Scotland in the mid 1700's

Paula Jones

Printed in the United States of America
ISBN 978-1-64133-930-8 (sc)
ISBN 978-1-64133-931-5 (e)
ISBN 978-1-64133-932-2 (hc)

This book is printed on acid-free paper.

2024.08.16

Blue Ink Media Solutions
1111B S Governors Ave
STE 7582 Dover,
DE 19904

www.blueinkmediasolutions.com

DALTON'S DREAM

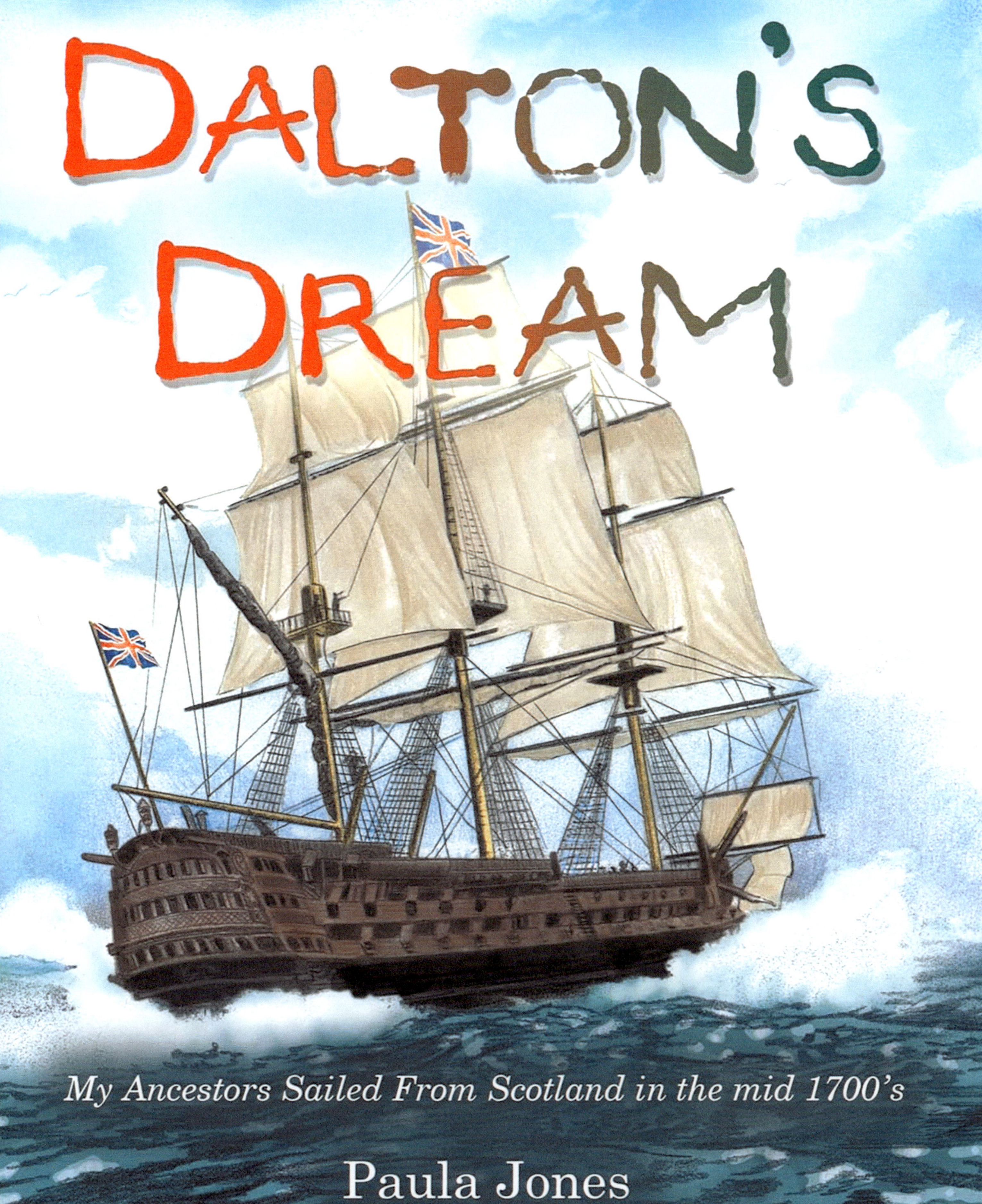

My Ancestors Sailed From Scotland in the mid 1700's

Paula Jones

You live as long as you are remembered.

Russian Proverb

*Knowing who our ancestors were is a bridge of
understanding to our past.*

Unknown

Introduction

My name is Dalton, and I want to tell you about my cool dream, when I met my ancestors.

It was the day after Christmas, and I was sitting on my living-room sofa, texting some friends about all the wonderful gifts I had gotten. My mother had given me my very own cell phone. Even though I had just had my twelfth birthday, I felt so grown up. I was glad that I was on Christmas vacation from school and that I could sleep late; however, this particular morning I sprang up out of bed with a burst of energy. The Florida sun was shining brightly through the window while I poured my orange juice. While looking out at the palm trees standing like soldiers, I was thinking it would be nice to celebrate Christmas someday where there was snow and I could build a snowman and go sledding. The Christmas-tree lights were still on and blinking like stars as I curled up on the sofa and texted some friends. While I was waiting for responses, I glanced at the family history book sitting on the coffee table. My Aunt Paula had written it. I picked it up and started slowly flipping the pages. Suddenly I came to a page about a twelve-year-old boy who was growing up in the early 1800s. Eagerly I continued to read. With each turn of the page, my head was filled with *OMG!* and *Wow!* The things I read in there made me instantly appreciate my mother, father, grandparents, and brother so much more, not to mention all the opportunities I had—especially my cell phone!

I fell asleep with the book resting in my lap. I dreamed I was transported back in time to Smithville, Tennessee, in the early 1800s. This was where my ancestors had settled when they'd sailed from Scotland to America. They were among the pioneers who helped shape the new world. There was no running water, electricity, bathrooms, cars, cell phones, iPads, iPods, televisions, Xbox games, skateboards, or any of the conveniences we have today. Life was hard and a challenge for daily survival; however, they were building a new life of freedom from the oppressive life they had left behind. They survived from the land and natural resources. They did everything for themselves, including growing their own food, making their own clothes, hunting, fishing, and cutting down trees to make their homes.

Come and let me take you on a great journey into my dream...

In my dream, I woke up suddenly to the sound of a gunshot and loud, rushing water. I looked around me in amazement. I didn't know where I was—but I knew it wasn't Florida. There was snow on the ground and lots of bare trees, with snow piled on the branches, and a partially frozen stream. I thought of Dorothy, in *The Wizard of Oz*, saying, "Toto, we're not in Kansas anymore." From across the stream, a young boy holding a rifle had spotted me sitting under the tree. I'm sure I stood out, with my bright-red soccer outfit and socks that I had put on earlier for practice. I would be an easy target as I stood out against the white snow, bare trees, and gray, cloudy sky. The boy crossed over the stream on a log, balancing himself with outstretched arms, holding his rifle in one hand and the turkey he had just shot in the other. He walked up the deep, snowy hill and just stood over me, staring, and I stared back. He was wearing torn pants and shirt, with suspenders peeking out from a heavy jacket, knee-high boots, and a fur hat with a raccoon tail. He looked just as amazed as I did.

Who was he, and where was I? After we broke our stare, I spoke first and asked his name. He said he was John Knox Bain, from Smithville, Tennessee. This was shocking, as I had just read in our family history book that John Knox Bain was my fourth grandfather, who had been born in 1827. I couldn't believe I was meeting him. We both continued to stare at each other, blinking our eyes and shaking our heads in disbelief.

John asked me what my name was and where I came from. I told him my name was Dalton Cole Wright and that I lived in Lakewood Ranch, Florida, which wasn't far from Tennessee. John said he has never left the farm, except to go into the local town of Nashville for some supplies. Then John asked what I had in my hand. I told him it was a cell phone my mother had given me for Christmas. "What's a cell phone?" he asked. I told him that when I wanted to speak with a friend who was not near me, I could push some buttons on the phone, which would connect me with my friend. Or I could text my friend a message. I tried calling my brother, Roman, to show John how it worked; however, I remembered there weren't any cellular towers—duh! John's eyes were wide, and he had a perplexed look on his face.

John picked up the turkey he had shot, and we began to walk through the family graveyard. He pointed out family members, especially those who had died in childbirth, which was common in those days due to lack of medical technology. I told him people who had died during the nineteenth century could be cured with a simple pill in my time. We had so many questions, and I was hoping I would not wake up before I had heard everything! I told John how I'd been reading my Aunt Paula's family history book and had fallen asleep to wake up sitting under a tree in the snow, when I'd heard the gunshot.

John was staring at my clothes. He informed me that only women wore colored clothing, and he laughed. I told him that boys wear all the colors of the rainbow, and it is the style in the twenty-first century; however, I was wearing my soccer uniform because I was going to practice for a tournament. He asked what the number fifteen was for, and I to d him that when we play soccer, each player has a number on his shirt.

He said it was his birthday, and I asked how old he was. He said twelve, and he told me he had killed the turkey for his birthday dinner. I asked what day and year it was, and he replied that it was December 1, 1839. I jumped back and said, "Wow... that's 161 years before I was born! My birthday is also December 1, but I was born in the year 2000. This is so cool• Our conversation was so energetic, and our questions kept overlapping. I was thinking that my mother and brother were going to wonder where I was. I was mesmerized, enjoying my dream, and was wondering when I would wake up.

DEWAR
McGREGOR

John asked me whether I was hungry, and I sure was. We crossed the open snowy field, which looked like a winter wonderland. I had never seen snow before. I saw icicles hanging from the trees as we headed for his log cabin, which I could see in the distance. We continued to fire questions at each other. I was still surprised that I didn't feel the cold. I told John, "Did you know I can tell your future ... who you will marry, and how many children you will have—and that you will enlist in the American Civil War in 1861, when you are thirty-four years old, along with your brothers?" John anxiously wanted to know more_ I continued, telling him, "A favorite family story is the one when you were responsible to hunt for food for your unit in the Civil War, and you went deep into the woods in heavy snow, hunting for squirrels. You only shot eleven, but you needed twelve for your unit. You shot one rat and cooked it with the squirrels, and no one ever knew. All the men praised you for a delicious meal. And in 1881, forty-two years from now, you will travel with your family by covered wagon from Smithville, Tennessee, to Hot Springs, Arkansas. That will take about four months, whereas in my day, it would only take about seven hours by car."

"What's a car?" John asked.

"It's an improvement on the wagon, only it moves without horses and mules. The wheels are covered with rubber, so it moves very smoothly, even over dirt roads and rocky terrain. It was invented in the early 1900s by Henry Ford. It goes very fast, and you get to where you're going much quicker than the days, weeks, or months it would take by wagon. There's so much that has been invented in the past 174 years: like the telephone, television, airplanes, and even people traveling to the moon in a rocket ship and landing on the moon." Well, John really got interested now, and he wanted to know how that was possible. I explained as much as I knew from my science teacher and books I had read and, of course, the Internet.

"Do you go to school?" I asked John.

He said, "No, but we have a schoolhouse next to our cabin, and my mother is the teacher. There are ten children in the class, of all ages. It's only one room and only girls. Boys are not required to go to school, as we are needed to help our fathers do the planting, harvesting, and hunting." I then asked if he played any sports. John looked confused and then shook his head to say no. Then he asked me whether I did.

I told him, "I'm on a soccer team, and my older brother, Roman, plays basketball."

John asked, "What's soccer and basketball?" We stopped, and I took a stick and drew an image in the snow to show him. He asked if we could play soccer after dinner. I was having so much fun and couldn't wait to tell Roman, my mother and father, and my soccer team. I was glad we were on Christmas break. I wouldn't have to worry about when I would wake up or whether I would be late for school.

We arrived at John's cabin, and I slowly went through the door, feeling very strange. My head moved in slow motion as I looked around the one large room with hand-hewn wooden floors, ceiling beams, a couple of beds made from logs off to the side, an open fireplace with a hanging kettle at the far end, and stairs leading to a loft. The cabin was completely made out of the local trees. It was a real log cabin like the one I had seen in our family history book. John handed the turkey to his mother, who was standing at a wooden table kneading biscuit dough, and introduced me. His father and brothers had gone into Nashville for supplies and would be returning soon. His two sisters were sitting in the corner, sewing. They all stared at me, and only the mother spoke. She asked John who I was and where I had come from. He explained to her that I had appeared in my dream and came from the twenty-first century. She had a perplexed look on her face, and it seemed too much for her to comprehend, but she welcomed me.

John told her that he was my fourth grandfather and that we had the same birthday and were both twelve years old today. A soft smile came across her face, and she went back to preparing the turkey. As I looked around the kitchen area, I was thinking of our kitchen in Florida, with all the convenient gadgets my mother had for cooking. Watching John's mother cook without running water and chop vegetables, I wished I could send over our plumber and give her a Cuisinart!

John took me upstairs to the loft to show me where he and his brothers slept. He had a fur hat with a raccoon tail hanging on his bedpost, which made me think of David Crockett. We sat and talked, watching the snow fall past the window. Since my brother, Roman, is sixteen and interested in girls, we don't have talks anymore, so I was enjoying talking with John. I thought about my very own room, with the walls covered with my favorite things and my own private bathroom. At the end of John's bed there was one pair of shoes, and there was no closet—only wooden hooks where his limited clothes were hanging. I thought that if he could see all the clothes and shoes Roman and I had, he would not believe it. I felt so fortunate to live in the twenty-first century. Then John wanted to show me the animals and wanted me to show him how to play soccer before dinner, so we went outside.

I had to duck my head when we went back down the stairs, or I would have surely bumped my head on the low beam. That might have wakened me from my dream, and I wasn't ready to wake up yet.

As we walked towards the door, John's mother was plucking the feathers from the turkey. She pleasantly smiled at me as I looked back while shutting the door.

There were animals in a small coral: a couple of pigs, some sheep, and lots of chickens. A stone well, with a bucket on a pulley, was where they got their water. There was no running water in the cabin, and no matter what the weather, someone had to get water from the well for cooking and bathing. I asked John where the bathroom was, and he pointed to a small outhouse with a carved moon on the door. It was such a contrast to my modern-day bathroom. They didn't even have toilet paper. As I looked down a deep, dark hole, I was glad I didn't have to sit down. There was only a bucket of leaves and a stack of catalogs. I thought of the soft Charmin toilet paper we took for granted. The air didn't exactly have the smell of Febreze air freshener!

"John, I've never seen snow before. Have you ever built a snowman?"

John eagerly replied, "No, but let's make one. "There certainly was a lot of fresh snow. I had seen people make snowmen in movies and story books, and I told John what we needed. We began to roll a large ball for the stomach, to rest on a slightly smaller ball for the base, and then a smaller ball for the head. We were having so much fun, we didn't even notice how cold it was. When the snowman was built, we had to give it arms, nose, mouth, buttons, and a scarf. I gathered some tree branches, and John got some coal from the open fireplace, a carrot from the kitchen, and a scarf that was hanging on his wall. When it was finished, I asked John if he had an old hat. He said there was one hanging on a nail in the barn, and he ran to get it. I took my cell phone out and took a picture of it. I showed John how to use the camera, and we took turns taking pictures standing next to the snowman. Now I knew what it was like to play in the snow and build a snowman!

I had a strange feeling that we had an audience watching us build the snowman, especially the squirrels that often hid from John's gun.

We walked to the schoolhouse and peeked in through the windows. I was standing on a big tree root that was actually growing into the schoolhouse wall. It was a small room, with wooden desks, a chalkboard with the vowels printed on it, a chair with a dunce hat on it, and a flag hanging on the wall. John asked me if I had ever worn a dunce hat and I said no, because I love to learn in school. But I explained that there are kids that didn't always behave in class and were sent to the principal's office, rather than having to wear dunce hats. I asked John what subjects his mother taught, and he said, "The three Rs: Readin', 'Ritin', and 'Rithmetic."

I told John that my school was made up of multiple buildings and that there were different rooms for different subjects and a different teacher for each class. I told him that my favorite subject was history, and that's why I was so thrilled to meet my ancestors. I could not wait to tell my history teacher when we went back to school after the holidays. I continued to be overwhelmed by the contrast between the early nineteenth century and the twenty-first century. It was amazing how much progress had been made in just 174 years. I was wondering whether John would be more shocked at seeing my life in 2013 than I was at seeing his in 1839.

As we were leaving the schoolhouse, a bird flew over our heads. I informed John that it was a mockingbird, which was the Tennessee state bird. It's difficult to see these songbirds sometimes because of their gray color. They can mimic other birds' calls, and that's why they're called mockingbirds. John appeared to be very hungry for the knowledge I was sharing with him. I couldn't imagine not being able to go to school, because I loved learning so much. I had a fresh awareness and appreciation of how important making good grades in school was for my future.

AE IOU
DUNCE

I asked John whether he wanted me to teach him how to play soccer. I looked around to see what we could use for a ball. There was a small pig hide hanging on the fence, so we stuffed it with leaves and bound it with string. I couldn't wait until I told my soccer team that I had taught my fourth grandfather, who was born in 1827, how to play soccer! I thought they would all think I was of my "soccer rocker."

John," I told him, "first you place your right foot on top of the ball, like this, and balance yourself with your arms outstretched. You are not allowed to use your hands, only your feet, to kick the ball. We'll use the fence as the goal." He got the hang of it right away. He was in great physical shape from all the work he did around the farm. "John, you'd make a great soccer player. I certainly would want you on my team," I said. At this he gave a big smile.

We were laughing as we saw John's father and brothers returning from Nashville. Seeing them on an old wagon being drawn by only one horse seemed very strange—nothing like my mother returning from the store in her car! As they approached the barn, where they would hitch the wagon, their eyes were wide open, and as soon as the wagon stopped, they jumped down, with the same surprised looks on their faces as their mother and sisters had had earlier. They looked me up and down, obviously surprised at the clothes I was wearing.

John introduced me, and all the brothers exchanged glances with each other and started to snicker at me. I understand teenagers, as my brother, Roman, is sixteen, and he teases me all the time. Some things never change with time. I found myself wishing that Roman were here so I could introduce him to them.

15

John's mother yelled that she needed some more wood for the fireplace. I could smell the cooking of the turkey coming from the chimney. John and I walked over to the woodpile. John picked up the ax and started chopping some wood into smaller pieces to fit into the fireplace. I asked if I could try it. It was fun, but I wouldn't want to chop wood every day. All the cooking was done in the open fireplace, and they needed lots of wood every day. That was just one of John's daily chores, he told me. Others were feeding the animals, gathering eggs, milking the cows, picking the chicken feathers for pillows and bedding, hunting and fishing, carving furniture, and building the wagons, pigpens, and fences. Death was a common occurrence in the lives of these pioneers, and John sometimes would carve the wooden boxes to bury them. He would dig the holes for the graves and carve the names on the headstones. I began thinking that I should help my mom more, as she works very hard.

I asked John what they did for bathing, since there was no running water in the cabin. He said they would go down to the river to bathe on Saturdays or special occasions, but during the winter they would heat water in the fireplace, fill a wooden tub, and take turns using the same water. I told John that that's where the saying came from: "Don't throw the baby out with the bath water"—because the water would be so dirty after being used by so many people.

I wanted to know what they did for fun. John said that in the summer, once a month, they would have a picnic after church, and the young children would play dress-up or hide-and-seek. He said sometimes he liked to climb his favorite tree and just be by himself, and sometimes he'd kill a squirrel with his slingshot and his mother would cook it. John was the youngest brother, and his friends lived too far away to see often. In the winter time, everyone was very quiet, he told me. The girls that went to school lived too far away to travel in the winter, so his mother only taught in the spring and summer. His mother and sisters quilted and made clothes, his dad carved com pipes and furniture, and he liked to carve toys for Christmas.

We took the wood into the house, and the smell of warm biscuits and turkey made my mouth water. I had not eaten any breakfast. The table was set with wooden plates, by John's sisters. John's father sat at the head of the table, and the oldest son sat at the other end. We sat down, and John's father said a prayer of thanks. I thought my family should start doing that too, as we had a lot to be thankful for—especially for living in the twenty-first century, where everything was so easy! While we waited for the turkey to finish cooking, we had so much to talk about. When the turkey was brought to the table, it was the largest turkey I had ever seen. It was delicious, although there was no dressing or cranberry sauce. Having enough to eat in the nineteenth century was sometimes a challenge due to crop failures, the weather, and the inability to preserve the foods, as they didn't have refrigeration. Everything had to be freshly killed, caught, or picked. In the future, when I open my refrigerator I'm going to appreciate having my favorite food right there when I want it—especially my chocolate chip ice cream!

The women of John's family did not enter into our after-dinner conversation. Women's opinions weren't respected. They always stayed in the background when there was company. They were to keep the house, cook, have children, and take care of them.

We remained at the table while the two sisters removed the dishes, and we entered into conversation as John's father lit a corn pipe. They had more questions for me than I did for them. Because my favorite subject in school was American history, I told them that I knew Martin Van Buren was their eighth president and had just been elected in 1837. I looked at John and told him that John Quincy Adams had been the sixth president when he was born, in 1827. They were very interested in what I had to say, because none of them had attended school. They spoke incorrect English, did simple writing, and spelled words as they sounded, which I had noticed from the gravestones when John and I had walked among them. "Died" was spelled "Dide" and sometimes the dates were reversed. They asked who the president was when I was born. "William Jefferson Clinton, in 2000," I said. "He would have been completing his second term in 2001. He was from Arkansas, like me. He was well liked, and everyone ailed him "Billy." His wife, Hillary, ran for President in 2009, against our first African-American President, Barack Obama. Obama won, and Hillary became secretary of state. She would have been the first woman to be elected as president. Obama, our forty-fourth president, was just elected for a second term and will go down in history as our first African-American president. At this, they all had looks of shock on their faces. In loud unison, they shouted, "A Negro President!"

"Yes," I said. "However, we don't call them Negros. They are African-Americans. Barack Obama was born in our fiftieth state, Hawaii. He had a white mother and a black father. He was educated in the United States and became a civil-rights lawyer and teacher before pursuing a political career. He was elected to the Illinois state senate in 1996 and elected president in 2008. He's a Democrat, which means he stands for the betterment of the common man."

It was difficult for John and his family to understand having a black president. Slavery was a major conflict and was still being practiced; slaves were sold and chained, without any human rights. The issue of slavery was such a volatile subject with Congress. I told them that in twenty-six years slavery would be abolished, in 1865, with the Thirteenth Amendment to the Constitution of the United States. And the sixteenth president, Abraham Lincoln, would be assassinated the same year at the Ford Theatre in Washington, DC, while he and Mrs. Lincoln were watching a play, Our American Cousin, written in 1858. They didn't believe me and could not imagine the future possibility. "History has already spoken," I said.

I noticed a tattered flag hanging in the comer, with thirteen stripes and only twenty-six stars. I went over, picked it up, and told them that our flag now had fifty stars but still had thirteen stripes, representing the original thirteen colonies. I told them how the US flag had evolved as the country grew and how each time a state entered into the Union a star had been added. "Do you know what the thirteen red and white stripes mean?" I asked. "The seven red stripes stand for 'Hardiness and Valor,' and the six white stripes stand for 'Purity and Innocence.' The blue background for the white stars stands for 'Vigilance, Perseverance, and Justice.' Also, your state of Tennessee was the sixteenth state to enter into the Union, forty-three years ago, in 1796." Sitting around the table, they listened intently and looked frozen with disbelief. I thought to myself, *I may end up being a history teacher some day.*

I kept thinking. *This is an incredible dream.* But as much as I was having such a cool experience, I did not want to remain in the early nineteenth century. I was wondering when I would wake up and see my family again. I was starting to miss them.

I knew I could not make a call on my cell phone, but I wondered whether I could take photos to show everyone when I returned to twenty-first-century Florida and shared my dream. I pulled the phone out of my pocket and held it up, and everyone looked like deer staring into headlights. I told them it was a camera as well as a telephone. I told them the first preserved portrait that existed would be taken later this month, called a "photograph" by Robert Cornelius. It meant "drawing by light." *Photo* means "light" and *graph* means "to draw." And the telephone would be invented by Alexander Graham Bell, in 1870, which would be another thirty-one years. I showed them that the cell phone was both a camera and a telephone. I took a picture of John with his father and brothers and showed it to them. They acted as though they had seen a ghost and looked at me as if I were a very strange young boy. I explained that our technology in the twenty-first century was very advanced. We took more photos, and I was just hoping that I had enough cell battery, as I didn't have my charger with me. I could not wait to show everyone these photos; it was a shame I couldn't make copies for John and his family.

Everyone was tired and got up from the table to go to bed. John said he had one last chore to do before going to sleep. He had to make sure the horses were covered in the barn and all the animals were inside. One of John's brothers, as he was walking up the loft stairs, looked back at me and said, "This was the most interesting winter evening we've ever had." Then he continued up the stairs, scratching his head.

While we were walking to the barn, each step we took broke through the frozen snow. I still didn't understand why I didn't feel the cold. Looking up at the clear, unpolluted sky, I saw a shooting star. "Quickly, John! Look up before it disappears! Make a wish," I said.

"I wish to have a dream like you and wake up in the twenty-first century and visit you in Florida." I pointed out the Big Dipper to him and told him that it was located in the Ursa Major (meaning big bear) constellation. "My favorite is the Orion constellation," I said. "You can only see it in the northern hemisphere during the fall and winter because in the spring and summer the image is blocked out by the brilliant sun." John said he would lie in the summer grass sometimes, looking up at the sky, and wonder what was up there. I told him that a spaceship had landed on the moon.

"What!" he said with a higher-than-normal voice. "You're kidding me, right?"

"No, it's true," I said. "A hundred and thirty years in the future, in 1969, two men named Neil Armstrong and Buzz Aldrin were the first men to land on the moon and actually walk on the moon. Our technology allowed us to hear what they were saying, millions of miles away. Neil Armstrong said 'One small step for man, one giant leap for mankind.' It was a very exciting time for America. From 1969 to 2013, in the forty-four short years leading up to my present day, space technology has developed space stations, where people spend months doing research and sending it back to earth.

"Mankind is destroying the earth with pollutants that come from factories and car fumes. Our skies are not as clear as yours. Space technology is working towards developing living conditions on another planet, as earth is becoming overpopulated. Our current world population is about seven billion. I read in our history books that in the early nineteenth century the world population was about 17 million, and you, John, are one of those 17 million. All the pollutants are destroying our wildlife, to the point of extinction, changing our weather and creating more frequent earthquakes and tsunamis." John said he had heard about earthquakes, but what was a tsunami? I explained. "It's a series of huge ocean waves, which sometimes reach over one hundred feet in height, crashing down on land, destroying anything in their path—people, buildings, and trees. It's generally caused by earthquakes or volcanic eruptions. There was a big tsunami in Japan in 2010 that killed thousands of people and destroyed their homes."

We continued to the barn, and I could hear all the animals, which sounded like a Dr. Doolittle orchestra. John had two favorite blade-and-white pigs, George and Martha, who were named after George Washington and his wife. They were the biggest pigs I had ever seen. I love animals, and it made me miss my dog, Susy, who had run away Christmas day. "John, do you have a dog?" I asked. "I haven't seen one around."

John said that he had had a big, long-haired gray dog, named Smokey, who had died a couple of months ago. We'd passed his grave this morning, he informed me. "My father wasn't too happy that I buried him in our family graveyard, but Smokey was my best friend," he shared with me.

John repeated his hopes to have a dream soon and come visit me in the twenty-first century. "That would be so cool," I said. "I would take you to a soccer game, and introduce you to my coach and team, and even let you play. You're in better shape than most of them. We'd go to the beach and to my favorite pizza and ice cream shop. You would love it!"

All of a sudden, while John was throwing a blanket over the horse, it reared up and knocked my cell phone out of my hand. As I bent down to pick it up, the horse kicked out and caught me in the head—and the next thing I heard was the electronic shutting of the garage door. My mother had just returned from food shopping. The contrasting image of John's father and brother returning from Nashville in a horse-drawn wagon ran through my mind.

I was glad I'd woken up at home again. I'd really missed my mother and brother, and I didn't want to miss soccer practice. I jumped up from the sofa and started telling my mom about my dream. I anxiously showed her the pictures I'd taken with my cell phone of John Knox Bain and his brothers and the snowman we'd built. She just laughed and continued to unpack the groceries. She thought the pictures were from the family album, but I told her that the pictures on my cell phone were not in the album. She said she would look later, that Roman had to take me to soccer practice now. Roman got the car keys, and while we were driving, I told him all about my dream and about meeting our fourth grandfather. He had no choice but to listen. He said he would look at the photos when he got home later. I told Roman how much I loved him and how lucky I was to have a brother like him. He smiled. Then he informed me, "You sure do talk a lot in your sleep."

Since waking from my dream, I look at things differently. I realize how important it is to help my mom more and not get angry when my brother teases me. And when I return to school, I know I will appreciate my teachers more. I will study harder to make good grades, as I know it will make a better future for me.

I hope John's dream comes true and he can visit me one day.

About the Author

Paula Jones always wanted to be a teacher, to share not only what was in books but also her own storehouse of knowledge and learning lessons in life that would support the choices of young people as they approach adulthood. After leaving the University of Arkansas in 1966, Paula moved to New York City, where she became interested in ancient art and had numerous opportunities to travel to areas of the ancient world. She moved to Miami Beach in 1984 and sold luxury real estate.

After attending several family reunions, she realized how important it was for our future generations to remember who their ancestors were. This inspired her to recently publish her family history and led her to write *Dalton's Dream* in hopes that, with each turn of the page, young adults reading it will have better appreciation for their parents. She also hopes they will appreciate the life they live in the twenty-first century and never forget the sacrifices their ancestors made for future generations.

Paula currently lives in Las Vegas, Nevada, where she recently retired from real estate and enjoying her "bucket list."